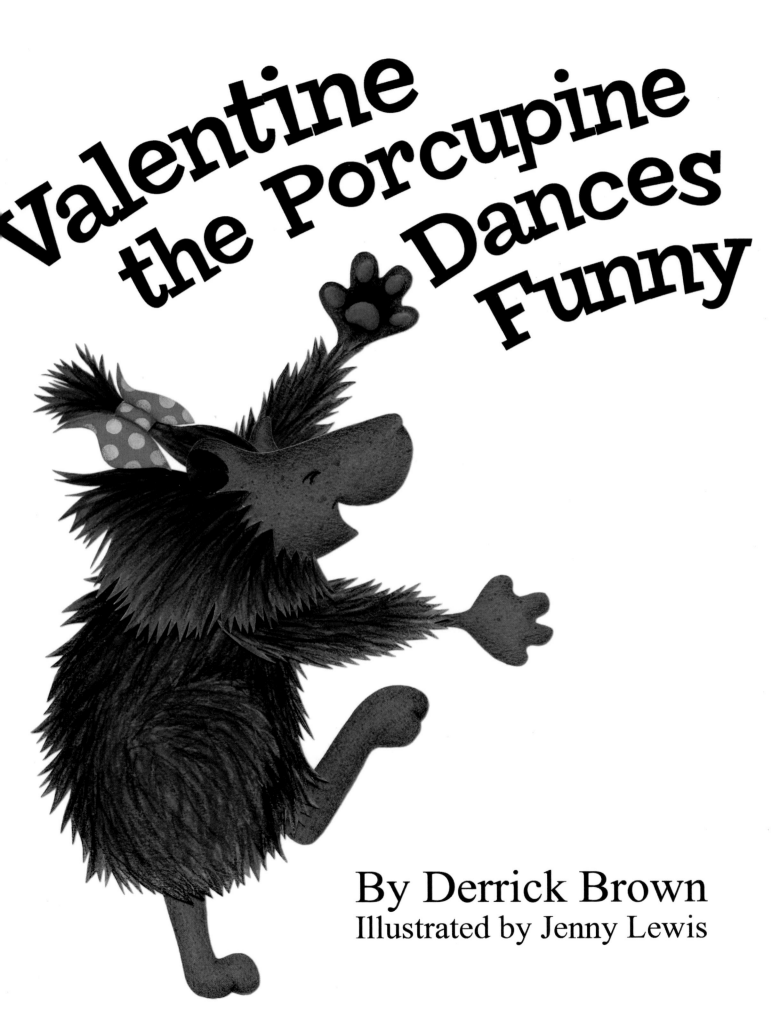

Valentine the Porcupine Dances Funny

By Derrick Brown

Illustrated by Jenny Lewis

Valentine the Porcupine Dances Funny
by Derrick C. Brown
Illustrated by Jenny Lewis

Write Fuzzy ©2011
1st Printing
Printed in Nashville, TN USA

Published by Write Fuzzy, Long Beach CA

Cover Design, Interior Layout and Illustrations by Jenny Lewis
Edited by Derrick Brown
Page photography by Nicole Caldwell
Type set in Chowderhead, Mongolian Baiti

To contact the author, send and email to brown@brownpoetry.com

writefuzzy.com

writefuzzy

the books we wished we had
when we were kids.

WRITE FUZZY
LONG BEACH, CA

Valentine the porcupine
danced without a care.

She danced inside the big bathtub

and while fixing her sticky, prickly hair.

She danced in front of people
and they whispered, "That girl is *strange*."

Momma said,
"Strange is cool, Valentine.
I hope you never change!"

Valentine said,
"I believe you, Momma!
I think strange can be cool, indeed.
It's going to be a strange day in my strange fur
under the strange, strange breeze."

Her Momma said,
"I love you because you are YOU, Valentine
You're the coolest kid in the world!
I hope that soon you find good friends
who can see you're a special girl."

Valentine grabbed her shoes
(the polka dot ones for dancing).
She hummed a tune and went to town
to pick out something fancy.

Would she buy
a dog shaped balloon
that chased clouds
shaped like bones?

Would she buy
a laser that gave
homeless people
homes?

Would she buy
some new shoes
that made her
float like a dove?

Would she buy
a magic dress
that made the
unloved feel loved?

The people of the town weren't always nice to Valentine.

"Valentine is just plain silly."

"Valentine is kooky."

"Valentine is willy-nilly
when she shakes her booty!"

Valentine never listened
to the mean things others said.
She just smiled and kept on dancing
in sparkly bows of red.

The townsfolk liked things boring
and were happy being dull.

Not Valentine!
She bought herself a beautiful boom box
with speakers shaped like skulls.

She went out into the world
to see all she could see.
"This world has so many people,
someone's got to dance with me!"

She met a bird, Mr. Burpyburg
who said he'd like to dance.

But when they got too close:
"OUCH! I just got poked!
And you ripped a hole in my pants!"

"Burrrrp. Chirrrp."

"You might just
have to dance
alone, kid!"

So Valentine was sad
and just wandered and wondered
if anyone would want to dance
and shake it.

She wondered if anyone would share their heart with her or if she would accidentally break it.

Valentine had just one dollar left so she walked into a shop.

SOMETHING FISHY

FREE

LAST
STRANGE
BLOWFISH

And just right there
in a bright fish tank
was a sight that made her stop.

She saw someone
with prickles
and pokers just as she.
The blowfish blushed
into a ball...

"You wanna dance with me?
How beautiful and strange!"
They looked into each other's eyes
and had a wonderful exchange.

Valentine said,
"I knew that if I waited,
I would find a special friend
to laugh between the butter flowers
and dance along the wind."

If you feel wild
and sometimes strange,
please don't be sad and blue.
A special friend is
somewhere waiting
to dance all day with you.

How to Make Friends

1. Say, "Hello" and smile. (Is there Peanut Butter in your teeth? You'd better fix that first.)

2. Ask if they have any pets. If they have a porcupine, be their friend forever!

3. See if you like the same things. If you like different things, that might be a BEST friend.

4. Try not to BURRRP or CHIRRRP.

5. When you say goodbye, a hug is nice. Squeeze them like a lemon and say, "I like your face!"